I want to keep warm at the park.
I am going to put on my warm clothes.

My socks are woolly.
My woolly socks
keep my feet warm.

I put on
my woolly jumper.
My jumper keeps
my body warm.

I want my coat too.
My coat is warm.

Now I put on my hat.
My hat keeps
my head warm.

My gloves keep
my hands warm.
I put on a scarf too.

Now I am going
to play at the park.
I look like a big
woolly ball!